The
Key Collection

Andrea Cheng

The
Key Collection

illustrated by Yangsook Choi

Henry Holt and Company

New York

Henry Holt and Company, LLC
Publishers since 1866
115 West 18th Street
New York, New York 10011
www.henryholt.com

Henry Holt is a registered trademark of Henry Holt and Company, LLC
Text copyright © 2003 by Andrea Cheng
Illustrations copyright © 2003 by Yangsook Choi
All rights reserved.
Distributed in Canada by H. B. Fenn and Company Ltd.

Library of Congress Cataloging-in-Publication Data
Cheng, Andrea.
The key collection / Andrea Cheng ; illustrated by Yangsook Choi.
p.   cm.
Summary: A ten-year-old boy in the Midwest misses his Chinese grand-
mother, who always lived next door until her health caused her to move.
1. Chinese Americans—Juvenile fiction. [1. Chinese Americans—
Fiction. 2. Grandmothers—Fiction. 3. Moving, Household—Fiction.
4. Old age—Fiction.] I. Choi, Yangsook, ill. II. Title.
PZ7.C41943 Ke 2003   [Fic]—dc21   2002068921

ISBN 0-8050-7153-9
First Edition—2003
Printed in the United States of America on acid-free paper. ∞

10 9 8 7 6 5 4 3 2 1

To Nicholas, with love
—A. C.

CONTENTS

The
Key Collection

CHAPTER ONE

The Letter

I could see Grandma Ni Ni's house from my bedroom window. If her light was on at night, I knew that she was reading her Chinese newspaper. Ni Ni saw my light too. Sometimes she told me in the morning, Xiao Jimmy, I think you stay up too late last night, and I'd say, I think you did too. That was our joke.

Monday morning my throat was sore. I got sore throats a lot, which I hated because my throat felt like it was on fire, but the good part was I could stay at Ni Ni's all day long. She put cool wash-cloths on my forehead and made me rice porridge with chicken broth. Then Ni Ni sat next to me on the sofa and rubbed my head until I fell asleep.

When I woke up, I was drenched in sweat. "Sweat makes fever go out," Ni Ni said. After that, I wasn't so dizzy anymore. We played rock-paper-scissors. Ni Ni used to play that a lot with her brothers when she lived in China. On the count of three, you made your hand look like a rock, a piece of paper, or a pair of scissors. Scissors beat paper. Rock beat scissors. Paper beat rock. I won ten times and Ni Ni won four. She said that was because her hands were old and my hands were young, but I thought it was just good luck. Then Ni Ni held my hands and said that she hoped I would always have good luck.

"I already do," I told her, "because your house is right behind ours."

Ni Ni smiled. "That is *my* good luck," she said.

When the mailman came, Ni Ni was disappointed that there were no blue airmail envelopes from her brothers in Shanghai, but there was a letter from my dad's sister, Auntie Helen, in San Francisco. Ni Ni opened it carefully so I could have the stamps for my collection. I watched her eyes as she read the tiny characters. When she got to the end of the letter, her eyes were far away.

"What does it say?" I asked.

Ni Ni didn't answer. I looked closely at the characters. The only one I could recognize was

xiao. Little. I was ten years old, but still everyone called me Little Jimmy. I wondered if they would call me that even when I was grown up.

"Ni Ni, can you teach me to write something in Chinese?" I asked.

Ni Ni took out a notebook with graph paper and wrote the character for *I* and the character for *you*. I practiced copying them into the squares. Ni Ni said I was making the strokes in the wrong order. She showed me again, but mine still didn't turn out like hers. Ni Ni looked disappointed, and I didn't want to keep practicing.

"English is easy," I said.

"For you," she replied. I knew English was hard for Ni Ni. She went to classes on Wednesday nights, but still my friend Jason couldn't understand a word she said. He thought she was speaking Chinese when she was speaking English. He didn't want to taste the *jiao zi* dumplings she made us for a snack, so I usually gave him a bag of potato chips instead.

Ni Ni put Auntie Helen's letter on the side of the counter and started to mix flour and water for our *jiao zi*. When the dough was ready, I made it into little balls and Ni Ni flattened them into circles with a wooden stick. She put meat filling in the middle with chopsticks, folded the circle in half, and pinched the edges together. I forgot all about my sore throat when I swallowed our *jiao zi*—with soy sauce and rice vinegar, it was the best lunch in the world. We made more than a hundred dumplings so I could take some home for dinner.

While Ni Ni washed the dishes, I looked at Auntie Helen's letter. The tiny characters were so perfect. I found the one for *I* and the one for *you* over and over again.

"Ni Ni, what did Auntie Helen write about *I* and *you*?"

Ni Ni dried her hands on her apron and sat down at the kitchen table. Then she pulled me close. "Auntie Helen wants me move to California."

"You already live here," I said.

"She thinks move there is better. I stay here in Cincinnati until you grow up, then go to Auntie Helen's in San Francisco."

"But I'm not grown up," I whispered.

CHAPTER TWO

Snow

I slept most of that afternoon. When I woke up, Mom and Ni Ni were talking in the kitchen while more *jiao zi* were steaming on the stove. My fever must have come back because the living room was spinning in circles and their voices were too loud. As soon as they saw I was awake, they stopped talking.

"Xiao Jimmy, do you feel better?" Mom asked. She came over to the sofa. Then I remembered Auntie Helen's letter. Mom touched my forehead. "Still a little warm," she remarked. Ni Ni put the dumplings into a container for us to carry home.

"*Xie xie*, thank you," Mom said. Then she asked Ni Ni to come to our house for dinner, but Ni Ni said it was too cold to go out. She would rather stay home. Why would she want to stay alone? Sometimes I was home before Mom and Dad, and it always seemed like the minutes took forever to go by.

We walked on the path from Ni Ni's back door to ours. It was snowing just a little, big wet flakes that melted on my jacket.

"Maybe we'll have a snow day tomorrow," I said.

"Maybe," said Mom. "We always get at least one snowfall in spring."

"Mom."

"Hmm?"

"Did Ni Ni show you the letter?"

"She did."

"She's not going to move, right?"

Mom stopped just before our back door. "I don't know, Xiao Jimmy. We have to talk it over with Dad. After all, Ni Ni is his mother."

⛎

Dad wasn't at all surprised by the letter. He said that Auntie Helen always wanted Ni Ni to move close to her, and lately she'd been more insistent. She was a doctor. Ni Ni had been having dizzy spells, and Auntie Helen wanted to keep an eye on her. Anyway, California was warm, and Ni Ni hated the cold. Even in spring she wore many layers to stay warm. Dad's voice was low and calm.

The *jiao zi* were now steaming in the middle of the table, but suddenly I wasn't hungry. The lump in my throat was so big that I could hardly breathe. Why didn't anyone tell me that Ni Ni had been planning to move? I'd never even heard about it. And what about the dizziness? Anyway, I was dizzy sometimes too. Like today I was dizzy most of the day. If Dad was a doctor like Auntie Helen, then he could run the tests for Ni Ni instead of designing buildings all day long. Of course Cincinnati was cold in the winter. But in summer it was so hot that even Ni Ni didn't wear sweaters.

I couldn't stop the tears from running out of my eyes and into my empty bowl. I pushed back my

chair and ran upstairs to my room, where I buried my face in my pillow.

Mom came up. Then Dad. They sat on the edge of the bed and tried to talk to me. Dad patted my head and said that I should think about what was best for Ni Ni, not what was best for myself. He said we could visit California someday. I wanted him to stop patting me. I wanted him to leave. Mom too. Everyone. Even Ni Ni. Dad said I was grown up now. I didn't listen to the rest of what he said. He called Ni Ni on the phone, but I covered my head with the pillow so I couldn't hear.

⚙

When I woke up in the middle of the night, I was wearing my pajamas. My clothes were in a pile on the floor, but I couldn't remember getting undressed. I glanced at the clock. Three in the morning. Ni Ni's light was on. I turned mine on too. Then I sat at my desk and practiced writing *I* and *you* with the strokes in exactly the right order. In the morning, I would show Ni Ni that I could write just like children in China. I would tell Ni Ni not to move. Then I remembered what Dad said. *Think about what was best for Ni Ni.* What about what was best for me?

I put my hands around my eyes so I could see better and looked out the window. Everything was covered with fresh snow: the locust tree, the bird feeder I had made for Ni Ni in first grade, the path between our house and hers. There were no footprints yet. I liked it that way, fresh and smooth.

Ni Ni turned her light off. I turned mine off too and crawled underneath my warm blankets. When

I woke up again, it was ten o'clock and the house was completely quiet. Mom had left me a note on the kitchen table.

No school today. Hope you feel well.
Ni Ni is waiting for you. I'll call later.
Love,
Mom

Just then the phone rang. I thought it would be Mom, but it was Jason asking if I wanted to shovel snow with him.

"For money?" I asked.

"Of course for money," he said.

"Sure. I guess so."

"Okay. I'll be right over."

Jason arrived before I had a chance to get my boots on. We decided to work our way down the block. Jason was much faster at shoveling than me. I could barely pick up the shovel when it was full, so I kept spilling snow on the part I'd already cleared.

"Do it like this," Jason said, showing me how to scoop the snow and dump it to the side. I tried, but my arms were so tired after we finished Mrs. Johnson's driveway that I had to sit down on the curb and rest. She gave us five dollars.

"How about we do your grandma's house next?" Jason said.

"I don't think so," I answered.

Jason looked surprised. "Why not? You don't think she's going to shovel all that snow herself, do you?"

I wasn't sure what to say. "No, I mean we can shovel it, but not for pay."

"Why not?"

"She's my grandma."

"Well, my grandma gave me twenty dollars to clean out the garage."

How could Jason take money from his own grandma? Suddenly I felt my dizziness coming back. "Anyway, I was sick yesterday and I think I still have a fever."

"So you're going in?"

I nodded.

Jason went over to the Donovans'. I watched him shovel for a minute. It looked so simple, the way he scooped the snow and flung it in one easy move. I wished I were big and strong like that. No matter how much I ate, I hardly grew at all. Dad said he was little like me in elementary school, but then he grew when he got older. He was sure I would grow someday too. But I wasn't sure at all.

Should I go home or to Ni Ni's? Nobody was at my house. The minute hand on the kitchen clock would take forever to move. I walked slowly through the snow to Ni Ni's front door. I turned the knob, but it was locked. Could she still be asleep? I remembered how late her light had been on. I knocked. No answer. I rang the doorbell over and over. Where could she be? Just as I was about to leave, the door opened and there was Ni Ni in her bathrobe. Her face looked sunk in. She hadn't put in her dentures, so her mouth folded in around her gums. She raised her hand to her face to hide it from me.

"Sorry, Xiao Jimmy, you see me like this. I think I caught something."

I followed Ni Ni to her room. She lay back against her pillow. "Maybe you caught it from me yesterday," I said.

"A little cold, that's all." She closed her eyes for a minute.

"Are you dizzy?" I asked.

"Little bit."

"I was too, yesterday," I said. "You were up late last night, Ni Ni."

She smiled weakly. "You too."

"I couldn't sleep."

"Me too." Then Ni Ni closed her eyes again and I tiptoed out of her bedroom. I fixed her a cup of tea with honey and lemon, but by the time I brought it to her, she was asleep.

CHAPTER THREE
Key Families

Auntie Helen's letter was still on the kitchen table. Next to it was a letter Ni Ni had started. She had lots of characters crossed out. Whole sentences, even. I saw my name a few times and the characters for *I* and *you*.

I picked up a Chinese dictionary from the shelf and looked through it. So many words to learn. Next to it was a big jar of keys. When I was little,

I used to fill my pockets with the keys and go around Ni Ni's house, pretending I was a janitor. It had been so long since I'd looked at them. I took the jar over to the rug, dumped the keys out, and buried my hands in their coolness.

I arranged the keys in one long row from big to small. Then I put them into key families. The Ni Ni key was an old silver one that was bent just a little. I picked another to be the Grandpa Ye Ye key. I had never met my grandpa, but Ni Ni showed me a picture of him. They had two kids, my aunt Helen and my dad. I picked two flat silver keys for them, and then a third one for Mom. The smallest key was me. I traced the character for *xiao* into the fuzz of the rug.

There were still so many keys left over. I picked four to be Ni Ni's brothers in Shanghai: Ming, Zhen, Rei, and Po. I knew their names from their

letters. Po was the youngest one. Ni Ni had played with him the most. She was right smack in the middle of the four brothers.

I heard the floor creak, and then Ni Ni walked slowly over to where I was on the rug and sat down next to me. "You the janitor, remember?" she asked.

I nodded.

"But now you are big," she said.

"Not really," I answered. "Not compared to Jason."

"Almost tall as me," she said.

"Are you still dizzy?" I asked.

"Better." Ni Ni sighed. She had put her dentures in, so her face seemed full again. Then she looked at the keys and picked up the little one. "This key is from the closet of my house in Shanghai. Once Po get mad. He lock himself in that closet. First just fine, sit in there in the dark. Then he hungry. Po always so hungry, so he tries open the door, but door is locked. He shouting and shouting for help, but nobody can open that door, even Ming cannot until I find key under the rug and set him free." Ni Ni started laughing. "I never forget his face when the door open. What he think, we leave him starve in there?"

"I bet he never shut himself in again."

"You don't know Po. He always cause trouble. Not big trouble, just little trouble."

"Still now?"

"Po never change," Ni Ni said. Then her eyes got that same faraway look as when she read Auntie Helen's letter. "Only now I don't know his trouble."

"He writes you letters."

"Yes, he writes. But I cannot hear his voice." Ni Ni put the key back in its place on the rug.

"Do you know what any of the other keys are for?" I asked.

"Don't know," Ni Ni said.

I scooped up the keys and started dropping them one by one back into the jar.

"Ni Ni, are you moving to California?"

Ni Ni held my hand in hers. "Auntie Helen already wait so long. She worry about me, Xiao Jimmy. She is doctor. Doctor knows best." I pulled my hand away, dropped the last key into the jar, and shut the lid tight.

CHAPTER FOUR

Getting Started

The whole next week, I didn't stop over at Ni Ni's. When I walked past her home, I turned my head the other way toward Jason's house. After school, I had potato chips and did my homework. Then I lay on my bed and read a book about the planets. Maybe someday I would be an astronaut. From up in space, you could look down and see the whole earth. You could even see the Great Wall of

China from way up there. You could watch the earth spin. Thinking about that made me feel dizzy. I thought about Ni Ni. Maybe she was dizzy too. I slipped on my boots and headed down the muddy path.

Ni Ni hugged me even before I was inside. She didn't seem dizzy at all. "Xiao Jimmy, still so cold and no jacket, you will get sore throat again."

I didn't hug her back. I bet Jason didn't hug his grandma. Anyway, sore throats were from germs. They had nothing to do with the weather. Ni Ni stepped back. "I made *jiao zi*," she said, "for after-school snack."

"How did you know I was coming?" I asked.

"I hope," she said. Ni Ni pointed to the pot already steaming on the stove. I looked around the kitchen. Everything was as cluttered as it always was. Newspapers were piled in the corner. Four aprons hung from a hook on the door. Strawberry baskets were stacked on top of the refrigerator. Ni Ni hadn't even started to pack. She sat down at the kitchen table and held her head in her hands.

"What's wrong?" I asked. "Are you dizzy?"

"No, not dizzy." Her voice got crackly. "But how can I start this moving? Your dad told me do nothing. He will hire movers. He will tell them put everything in boxes for me, but, you know, Xiao Jimmy, everything not so simple." Ni Ni pulled her fingers through her hair. "Not so simple."

I wanted to tell her that she didn't have to move. Nobody would make her. We could explain to Auntie Helen that she wasn't ready. Not yet. Not for a long time.

Ni Ni went over to the sink and started putting away the dishes in the drying rack. She put the bowls inside the cabinet. When she placed the last

one on top of the stack, the bowls came crashing to the floor and exploded all over the kitchen. For a minute I just stared at the pieces of blue and white. Ni Ni was frozen in the middle of the mess. She didn't say a word.

"I'll get the broom," I said, stepping carefully over to the closet. Ni Ni watched as I swept. Finally when all the pieces were in a pile, she sat down.

"Yesterday I break a glass, then try to clean it up, cut my hand," Ni Ni said. She showed me her palm. There was a deep red line across the middle.

"Maybe you need stitches," I said.

Ni Ni shook her head. "Not so bad, Xiao Jimmy. Just old lady has thin skin."

I swept the pile into the dustpan and carefully placed the large pieces in the garbage. Then I used the vacuum cleaner to pick up the tiniest pieces.

Ni Ni stared out the window while I worked. When I was all done, I looked around her small kitchen. "Well, I guess we can start up here," I said, climbing onto the counter and taking down the green baskets.

"Start?"

"Start going through your things before the movers come," I said.

"Careful, Xiao Jimmy, don't fall," Ni Ni said.

"Think we can throw these away?" I asked.

Ni Ni took the baskets from me. "You know, Xiao Jimmy, when I was little girl, my parents have so many children and not enough anything, so Mother told me, 'Xiao Mei, you save everything. Maybe someday you need it.' So still now, I cannot throw away." I tried to imagine Ni Ni as Xiao Mei, little sister.

"Ni Ni."

"Hmm."

"When did everyone stop calling you Xiao Mei?"

"Stop?" Ni Ni smiled. "My big brothers call me Xiao Mei now."

"But you're almost eighty!"

"They are eighty-two, eighty-four."

"What do your younger brothers call you?"

"They say Jie Jie, big sister."

"So you have two names."

"You forget one name," Ni Ni said, taking my hands.

"*Ni Ni*," I said, and smiled.

Then Ni Ni counted on her fingers. "Anyway, I have secret. I am almost eighty, but only have one birthday."

"Only one?"

"Because I born on special, what do you call it, special leap year. Only once every sixty years. Use lunar calendar."

"So your birthday comes only every sixty years?"

Ni Ni nodded. "So really I am only one and a third." She laughed.

"So you are Xiao Ni Ni and I am Big Jimmy."

※

My arms were tired from cleaning the tops of the cabinets. Ni Ni said we did more than enough work for one day. While we ate the *jiao zi*, Ni Ni told me all about the lunar calendar and the Chinese zodiac. She wrote down the different animals and the years that went with them on a napkin.

Turns out I was born in year of the monkey and she was born in year of the boar.

A little later, Jason came to the door. "Hey, Jimmy, want to play?" he asked. I didn't really. What could I say? That I was busy learning about the Chinese zodiac? Jason would think that was even stranger than the *jiao zi* we ate. "What are you doing?" Jason asked, glancing at the napkin.

"My grandma's showing me the Chinese zodiac. I was born in year of the monkey, but you're four years older, so you're year of the dragon."

"I am?" Jason asked if he could copy down the animals and the years. Ni Ni gave him a piece of paper and a pencil. "My sister's year of the snake," he said.

"Good year, year of the snake," Ni Ni said.

Jason understood her English this time. "I'll tell her," he said. "Hey, are you guys spring cleaning?"

He pointed to the bags and baskets on the kitchen counters.

"Not exactly," I answered. "My grandma's moving."

"She is? Where to?"

"California. My aunt lives there."

"Way out there?" Jason looked surprised. "I've never even been past Indiana." Jason folded up his paper. "So, you want to come out and shoot some baskets?"

I thought for a minute. I wasn't good at basketball. I hardly ever hit the backboard. But if I always said no, he would stop asking. Then, when Ni Ni was gone, what would I do?

"Sure," I said, pushing back my bowl.

"Tell your grandma thanks for the zodiac. Oh, and tell her if she needs help with the moving, I'm pretty strong."

Why didn't Jason tell her himself? She could understand if he spoke slowly. Why did he always say things right in front of her like she couldn't hear?

"We're going out," I said to Ni Ni.

"Have fun," she replied in almost perfect English.

CHAPTER FIVE

Sorting

The next day after school, Ni Ni and I sorted through her stuff. Things like extra sheets and towels went to charity. A broken watering can went into the garbage pile. Sometimes we argued about what was garbage and what wasn't. Ni Ni put faded old curtains into the charity pile.

"Nobody wants them," I said.

Ni Ni held up the fabric. "See this part here?

No holes. Somebody can cut two small dresses. Three little shirts. Cut around faded part, Xiao Jimmy." Ni Ni folded the fabric into a neat rectangle and put it on top of the ironing board. "I will iron it first," she said, smoothing the wrinkles.

Sometimes Ni Ni forgot we were sorting and started reading articles from the Chinese newspapers she'd cut out so long ago that they were yellow. "This article interesting for you, Xiao Jimmy," Ni Ni said. "Every day, you do eye exercises." Ni Ni showed me how to rub my temples in slow circles and then move down to my eyeballs. "That way, eyes won't be tired." Ni Ni said that when she was in elementary school, they did eye exercises and regular exercises every day before they started their lessons. Ni Ni pushed the kitchen table against the wall so we both had room to move our arms in circles. "Like this," she said, counting slowly to eight. "*Yi, er, san, si, wu, liu, qi, ba.* Then start over again."

While we were circling our arms, Dad stopped in. Ni Ni dropped her arms quickly. "Xiao Jimmy learning Chinese exercises," she explained.

"That's great," Dad said, but he wasn't really listening. "The movers are coming a week from today."

"One week?" Ni Ni asked.

Dad nodded. March 25. Then he started moving things around very quickly. He didn't ask Ni Ni about the piles. He just took a whole stack of newspaper articles and put them in the trash can.

"But Ni Ni hasn't looked through those yet."

"Look, Jimmy, there's only one more week. We've got to get this stuff sorted out." His voice was loud. "Why don't you go outside and play?"

First Dad said I was grown up, so Ni Ni could

move away, and now he was saying that I was too little to help. Didn't Dad care that his own mom was moving more than two thousand miles away? He said we should think of what was best for Ni Ni. Was throwing away all the articles that she had saved for so long best? I felt the lump in my throat again. Dad was taking pile after pile to the garbage. Sweat was pouring down his face and soaking into the neck of his T-shirt.

Dad went to the sink and filled two glasses with water and ice. He set them on the table and motioned for me to come over. I hesitated.

"Sorry, Jimmy," Dad whispered. I sat down and drank the water in little sips. "You know, this is hard for everyone." We looked over at Ni Ni. She was taking the articles one by one out of the trash and sorting them into piles. Dad finished his glass of water, stood up, and glanced around the kitchen.

"Thanks for helping, Jimmy." He started wrapping Ni Ni's serving bowls in newspaper.

"Wait," said Ni Ni. "Not that newspaper. Not finish reading that one. Here, you use this one." She handed Dad an old Cincinnati paper. Dad unwrapped the bowl, smoothed out the crumpled Chinese newspaper, and handed it to Ni Ni.

卍

Today the air was cool, but the spring sun was warm. A few patches of snow were melting in the driveway. Jason dribbled the ball and took a shot from the end of the blacktop. It hit the rim and bounced out. I tried from closer and completely missed the basket. Jason showed me how to push the ball from underneath. I hit the backboard the second time, and the third time I made a basket.

"Two points," said Jason, giving me a high five. "So, your grandma's moving to California."

"Yup."

"I wonder who'll move into her house."

Then it hit me. Somebody else would cook at Ni Ni's stove. Somebody else would wash dishes at her sink. Whose light would I see in the window at night?

"Maybe there'll be a kid our age," Jason said.

"I don't know."

"*Yes!*" said Jason as his ball swished through the basket.

We shot baskets for a long time. Once in a while, I got one through. Mostly they bounced off the rim. After a while, we sat down on the curb. "Want to come down to my house?" Jason asked. "We've got a Ping-Pong table."

I shook my head.

"Why not?"

"I have to help my grandma."

"Your dad's already helping her."

"I know, but she's only got one more week."

Jason shrugged. He wiped the sweat off his face with his shirt and stood up. "You know, Jimmy, you . . ." Jason dribbled the basketball a few times. "Never mind." Then he headed down the street toward his house.

What was Jason going to say? That I was strange? Weird? From another planet? What could I tell him? That I'd never played Ping-Pong? That I was probably worse at that than I was at basketball? Jason looked back at me just before he opened his front door. I could have waved. I could have said, "Wait, I'm coming." Instead I watched his front door open and shut.

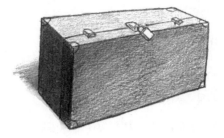

CHAPTER SIX

Packing

Only one more day until the movers would load everything into the truck. Ni Ni's house was so full of piles that it hardly seemed like hers anymore. We ran out of boxes, so Dad had to go buy some more. They came in flat stacks, and Ni Ni asked me to fold them into boxes. I tried to bend the cardboard where the lines were, but my box wasn't quite square, so the lid didn't fit. When I attempted to straighten it out, the cardboard tore. Dad took it from my hands.

I looked around. Maybe I would go home and read my book upstairs in my room. Or I would go out and shoot baskets. If I practiced more, I'd get better. Then I saw the jar of keys on the floor, not yet packed into a box. I picked it up and headed down to the basement, where I didn't have to see all of Ni Ni's bowls and chopsticks buried in layers of newspaper.

I dumped out the keys on the small rug by the washing machine. I found the Xiao Jimmy key that Ni Ni had used to rescue Po. What about the others? Were they keys to other closets in Shanghai? Other houses in China? Were some keys to this house?

My stomach growled. I hoped for a minute that Ni Ni would make *jiao zi* for lunch, but I knew there wasn't much time. Anyway, Ni Ni had already packed the wooden stick that we needed to flatten the wrappers. How could we roll out the dough without the stick?

Dad came down the stairs, carrying a trunk so big that I could hardly see him behind it. "Be careful," Ni Ni said. "Too heavy. Might hurt your back." Dad set the trunk down in a corner of the basement near the door. Then they hurried back upstairs.

I arranged the keys into families again. I moved the Ni Ni key around from Shanghai to Cincinnati to San Francisco. I did eenie meenie minie mo. The Ni Ni key landed on Auntie Helen.

Suddenly the big trunk caught my eye. I didn't remember seeing it before. What could Ni Ni keep in that big trunk? I stepped over the boxes and pulled on the lid, but it was locked. I scooped up all the keys and tried each one in the hole. The fat keys didn't fit in. The flat ones went in easily and turned around, but they wouldn't open the lock. What about the Ni Ni key? It was bent, but it still fit into the keyhole. It turned once and then again. I heard a click, and the latch sprang open.

The lid was heavy. Inside the trunk I saw the brightest, shiniest blue fabric I had ever seen, covered with embroidered butterflies. It was a big quilt. I spread it over the basement rug and lay down. Then I arranged the keys on the blue silk. The butterflies were flying all around the keys.

Ni Ni came down the basement stairs. "Xiao Jimmy, I have job for you," she said. She looked around for me. When she saw me lying on the quilt, she didn't say anything. Then she came over and sat down next to me.

"It was in the trunk," I said.

"How you open that trunk, Xiao Jimmy?"

I held up the bent key.

"So many years ago." Ni Ni traced one of the butterflies with her finger. "I even forget where I put it. When I decide to leave China, my mom made this quilt for me. Butterflies, she say, because she want me fly, but stay warm too."

"Ni Ni, do you really have to move to California?"

Ni Ni didn't answer. We just sat for a long time even though the movers were coming soon. I showed Ni Ni the key families. I told her how I did eenie meenie minie mo and she landed on Auntie Helen. We did it over again with the Xiao Jimmy key. First it landed on Mom and Dad, and then on Auntie Helen, and then on my great-uncle Po in China.

"Xiao Jimmy key go everywhere," Ni Ni said.

"Even to Uncle Po in China."

"Even Uncle Po."

"I never met him."

"He still knows you. I write everything. He knows you like keys."

"He does?"

"He has keys waiting for you in Shanghai."

My stomach growled so loud that Ni Ni said Po could probably hear it across the ocean. "How about we make *jiao zi*?" Ni Ni suggested.

"But the kitchen is packed."

"What is packed can unpack."

"Dad is in a hurry to finish."

"But Dad is hungry too."

I made the dough into balls, and Ni Ni rolled it with the stick. We both put the filling in the middle. Ni Ni showed me how to pinch the edges, and after the first few, mine looked just about right.

CHAPTER SEVEN
Leaving

I didn't want to watch the movers carry all the boxes into the truck. Neither did Ni Ni, but we couldn't think of what else to do. It was damp and chilly, so Ni Ni had on four sweaters, and still she shivered.

The movers were fast. In just over an hour, Ni Ni's house was completely empty. Mom fixed hot noodle soup at home for lunch, but Ni Ni hardly touched hers. She just held her glass of tea in her hands. Mom said there was a real estate agent who would clean the house and put it on the market. Ni Ni nodded, but I could tell she wasn't listening.

The doorbell rang. There was Jason with a plate of chocolate chip cookies. "These are from my mom," he said, handing me the plate. Then he just stood there, not knowing what to say.

"Thanks," I said. "Do you want to come in?"

He glanced around quickly. Mom and Dad and Ni Ni were sitting around the dining-room table with their noodles. You could smell the shrimp Mom had added at the last minute because it was Ni Ni's favorite. Jason wrinkled his nose. "No thanks. You want to come down to my house?"

"We're going to the airport in a little while," I said.

"When you get back, come on over."

"Okay," I agreed, thinking that I'd come up with an excuse later on. Until now, I always said I was going to my grandma's, but when she was gone, what would I say? Too much homework?

While Mom cleaned up, Ni Ni worked on a thank-you note to Jason's mother. First she wrote it in Chinese characters. Then I helped her with the English. She copied it over onto scrap paper and finally onto a small thank-you card that Mom had on her desk.

Dear Jason and Jason's Mom,
Cookies are so delicious.
Thank you very much. I miss you.
Jimmy's Grandma

On the envelope she wrote, *To Jason and Mother*. We walked down the street to deliver it, but nobody was home, so we left the card in their mailbox.

Ni Ni stood in front of Jason's house, looking over at her own. "So many years," she said. Even though it was still daylight, the moon was almost full, just rising behind her house. Ni Ni took my hand. "When I leave China, my mom says to me, 'Xiao Mei, when you see moon at night, that is the same moon I see, so we see each other in that moon.'"

"I will tell the moon if you stay up too late," I said.

"I will tell the moon too," Ni Ni said, squeezing my hand.

❊

The airport was crowded. Ni Ni only had a handbag with two sweaters for the trip. Everything else was in the moving truck. We had a whole hour before the flight left. Mom tried to ask us questions, but nobody felt much like answering. Ni Ni kept checking to make sure she had her ticket. Then Dad noticed the cut on her hand. "How did that happen?" he asked.

Ni Ni looked at me. "Only small cut," she said.

"But how did you cut yourself?"

"I break a glass," she said.

"Her skin is thin," I explained, "so she gets cut easily."

Dad shook his head.

When it was time to board the plane, Ni Ni stood up unsteadily. I took her arm. "Are you dizzy?" I asked.

"Not dizzy, Xiao Jimmy," Ni Ni said. "Not dizzy, just old."

"But you are only one and a third, remember?"

"I remember." Ni Ni smiled a little.

Mom and Dad said good-bye, and I walked with Ni Ni as far as I could go without a ticket. Then she stopped and looked around in her handbag. Where was the ticket? She handed me the black bag. I looked in the zippered pocket. There, in an envelope labeled with Chinese characters, I found the ticket and handed it to Ni Ni. She tried to give it to the lady at the counter, but the lady pointed to the ticket counting machine. "It goes in there," I said.

Ni Ni was unsure. She tried to put the ticket in upside down. I took the ticket, turned it around, and fed it through the slot. Then I handed the stub to Ni Ni. "Keep this part," I said. There were

lots of people waiting to board the plane. Some of them were glancing at their watches. "You better go," I added.

Ni Ni looked at all the people. She squeezed my arm. Then, without once turning back, she walked unsteadily down the ramp.

CHAPTER EIGHT

The First Night

My clock said four. From habit, I looked out the window of my room that faced Ni Ni's house. No light. Then I remembered. Ni Ni was already in California. I buried my face in my pillow. Maybe it wouldn't work out. Maybe Ni Ni would call and say that California was too hot and she wanted to come home. I would tell Mom and Dad to wait on selling the house. Sometimes you planned things one way and they turned out another. Like Mom said they'd bought our house because it had a street full of kids for me to play with. Then it turned out that most of the kids moved away, except Jason. Mom thought Jason was a good boy. She always asked "Why don't you go out and find Jason?" whenever I said I was going over to Ni Ni's.

Four-fifteen. One-fifteen in California. Ni Ni was probably still awake. Maybe the light was on in her window at Auntie Helen's. I would have to ask her which way the window faced. I looked for the moon, even though it was dark outside. I tried to go back to sleep, but I couldn't stop remembering Ni Ni at the airport. Finally I got up and went down to the kitchen.

Dad was sitting at the table. His eyes were puffy. "I couldn't sleep," he said when he saw me.

"Me either."

Dad pulled one of the chairs closer to his. I sat down stiffly. Neither of us said anything. I picked up the salt shaker and turned it around in my hands. "You wanted Ni Ni to move, didn't you?" I said finally.

Dad tried to pat my hair, but I pulled my head away.

"You wanted her to move," I repeated, and my voiced choked up. That was always my problem. The minute I tried to say anything, I cried. In second grade, the kids called me a crybaby, and they were right.

"Ni Ni decided," Dad said quietly. Then he took off his glasses, rubbed his eyes, and began to

speak. "When I was little, my father used to try to tell Ni Ni what to do or not do, but it never worked. He tried to tell her that they should stay in China and that things would get better there. But Ni Ni had already decided. She wanted to come to America."

Why was Dad telling me all about things that happened long before I was born? What did leaving China have to do with now? I wanted to block out his voice, cover my head with my pillow, but my pillow was upstairs on my bed. Dad continued.

"Even Ni Ni's mother begged her not to go, but her mind was made up." Then Dad got quiet, and when I looked at his puffy eyes, there were tears in the corners.

"Is that when her mother made Ni Ni the butterfly quilt?" I asked.

Dad nodded.

My stomach growled. Dad put his glasses back on, stood up, and put some water into a pot. When it boiled, he added two packages of noodles. "I know it's not *jiao zi*, but it's the best I can do," he said. Just as the sun was rising, Mom came in. She sat next to me and touched my arm. Dad served us the noodles, and we all ate them together.

CHAPTER NINE

New Neighbors

$\mathcal{T}$wo weeks later, the real estate lady put a FOR SALE sign in Ni Ni's front yard. Why did they have to make the sign so big when the house was so small? She also put two pots of pansies on the front steps. Ni Ni never had flowerpots on the steps.

The lady called out to me. "Your grandma forgot a few things," she said, handing me a bag. Inside was a silk scarf, a chopstick, and the whole jar of keys. Suddenly I realized that I had left the jar by the washing machine. How could I have forgotten about the key collection? "Looks like you've got quite a few keys there," the lady said with a smile.

I nodded.

"I guess I do too," she said, taking a huge ring of keys out of her purse.

"Do you know what they're all for?" I asked.

"Yes, they're all labeled. Except I do have one key that I'm not sure about." The lady took it off the ring. "Here. How about you add it to your collection?"

The key was small, with the top shaped like a four-leaf clover. A good-luck key. I put it into the jar. "Thanks. Thanks a lot."

Jason came by on his bicycle. "Want to shoot some baskets?" he asked.

Basketball was getting a little easier for me. Every now and then I managed to make some shots even from the end of the driveway. "Okay," I said, setting the jar of keys on my front porch.

"What's that?" Jason asked, pointing to the keys.

"Just a bunch of keys," I answered.

"To what?"

"I don't know."

"What do you keep them for, then?"

I thought of trying to tell Jason that the keys were good for lots of things, that there were whole key families in that jar. Instead I just shrugged.

While we were shooting baskets, a car pulled up. A man and a lady holding two little boys got out and went into Ni Ni's house.

"Maybe they'll buy it," Jason said.

"I hope not."

"Why? Don't you want them to?" Jason asked.

"I don't want kids tearing up my grandma's house."

"Well, somebody's got to buy it." Jason was right. What difference did it make anyway? "If they have kids, I bet we could get some baby-sitting jobs." I hadn't thought of that. Jason was almost fourteen, old enough to really baby-sit. I'd be better at baby-sitting than shoveling snow. Suddenly I had an idea. "I wonder how long it would take to earn the money for an airplane ticket to California."

"By the end of the summer, I bet you'd have enough," Jason said. He sat down on the curb. "Hey, we could be a baby-sitting team."

"Jason and Jimmy's Baby-sitting Service," I said.

"J and J's," Jason said. He put out his hand and

I slapped it. "J and J's Baby-sitting Service, the best in town!"

⌘

Ni Ni's house sold in less than a week. Two days after Dad signed the papers, there was a big moving truck in front of it. The movers unloaded about fifty boxes, two cribs, a high chair, and a huge stuffed bear.

"Guess they do have kids," Jason said.

"Looks like a lot of them. I can't believe all that stuff is going to fit in my grandma's house."

Jason's mom called him from their front porch. "I gotta leave. We're going to my grandma's in Indiana today for spring break." Jason didn't look too happy.

"What's wrong with that?" I asked.

"There's nothing to do. If we sit on the sofa, my grandma says we're messing it up. If we open the fridge, she tells us not to eat this or that." Jason's mom called again. "See you later."

I watched Jason hurry to get in the car, where his mom and his sister were waiting. He acted as if he didn't like his grandma. If only Ni Ni had moved to Indiana instead of California. Then I could go visit her there.

I walked back to my front porch, picked up the jar of keys, and put my hand all the way to the glass at the bottom. What was I saving the keys for anyway? Jason was right. They weren't good for much. So many keys to nothing.

Mom introduced herself to the new neighbor, whose name was Alice. She was holding twin baby boys, one in each arm. Mom patted their heads, and they stared at her face with their big blue eyes.

"Must be quite a handful," Mom said.

Alice sighed. "Sometimes I think I need four more hands just to keep after them." The one named Rob struggled out of her arms. She put him on the floor, and he crawled over to one of the big boxes and tried to get on top of it. The other one, Mark, had his little hands tangled up in her hair. Suddenly he stopped pulling, looked at me, and reached his arms toward me.

"Well, that's a first," Alice said, handing him to me. "Looks like you've got a way with little ones."

Mom smiled. "Jimmy is just starting to baby-sit," she said.

"Well, I think we bought the perfect house,

then," Alice said, grabbing Rob just before he toppled backward off the box. She tried to take Mark from me, but he started crying.

I spent most of the afternoon helping Alice with the boys so she could unpack a few boxes. I told her about how Ni Ni used to live in the house, but now she was in California because my aunt was a doctor, and she was going to keep an eye on her.

Alice nodded. "Tell your grandma that we love her little house," she said. Suddenly we saw that Rob had something in his chubby hand. "What did you find?" Alice asked him. He held something out to me. "Is this yours?" I asked, showing Alice a dusty key. She looked at it closely. "Not mine," she said. "Must be your grandma's." I put the key in my pocket for later.

At home, I rinsed the key off and put it in the jar. For a while, I had no new keys to add to the collection, then I got two in one week. Things seemed to work like that. Nothing for a long time and then everything at once. I wrote to Ni Ni all about Rob and Mark and the two new keys. At the end I wrote, *P.S. The moon told me you are staying up too late.*

※

Every day I waited for a letter from Ni Ni. Mom said the mail service was slow and that I should give Ni Ni time to get settled, but after two weeks, there were still no letters. We called Auntie Helen's. Ni Ni's voice was thin and far away. "Do you like California?" I asked.

"I like," Ni Ni answered.

"Is it warm?" I asked.

"A little bit warm," she said. She seemed in a

hurry to hang up. "I write a letter soon, Xiao Jimmy," she promised.

Ni Ni's first letter was addressed to me. Ni Ni had used special year of the horse stamps. I used a flat key to open the envelope without damaging them. The note was short. Ni Ni said that the weather was a little chilly in California. She said that she was glad the new neighbors liked her house. She wrote all that in English. I remembered how hard it was for her to write the thank-you card to Jason and his mother. It must have taken her a long time to write the letter. At the end she wrote a sentence in Chinese characters. I could read the *I* and the *you*, but I couldn't read the one in the middle. "That means 'miss,'" Mom said.

CHAPTER TEN

An Invitation

Jason and I baby-sat for Rob and Mark three afternoons a week so Alice could get things done around the house. Mark loved balls, so usually Jason took him outside. Rob liked me to read him books. Alice paid us each three-fifty an hour because she said twins were double trouble. I put my money in a coffee can that I kept on my shelf next to the key collection.

When I got home Monday, first thing I did was check the mail, but there were no new letters from Ni Ni. Mom said she was probably still busy unpacking, but I didn't think so. I wondered what Ni Ni did all day. When she lived in her old house, mostly she cooked and cleaned. Did she clean Auntie Helen's house? Did she make *jiao zi*? Did she write letters to Po in China? Did she forget about writing to me?

On Wednesday, Rob was fussy all afternoon. When I offered to read him a book, he said, "Bad book," and threw it on the floor. I took him outside, but Mark wouldn't give him a turn with the ball, so he cried. When I took him in, he scratched my eye. By the time Alice came downstairs, Rob was asleep in my arms, but I was exhausted.

Mom and Dad weren't home yet. There was a letter in the mailbox from California, but it wasn't addressed to me. The handwriting was Auntie Helen's.

I emptied the money can onto the rug. I stacked the dollar bills. Twenty dollars so far. How much was a ticket to California anyway? Must be over two hundred dollars. I figured that even by the end of the summer, I wouldn't have enough. Maybe it wasn't worth it to keep on baby-sitting. I looked at my eye in the mirror; it was sore and red.

My stomach growled. If Ni Ni were still in her house, I could go see her and we could make the *jiao zi* dough together. I dumped out the keys and mixed them around on the rug. I picked up the one that Rob had found. It looked old. Maybe it had belonged to somebody who owned the house before Ni Ni. I put the keys into families again.

Where should the four-leaf-clover key go? I added it to Po's family.

When Mom came home from work, she saw Auntie Helen's letter on the table. She read it lots of times. "How's Ni Ni?" I asked.

"Auntie Helen says she hasn't had any more dizzy spells. Auntie thinks maybe that was just a temporary inner ear problem that cleared up by itself."

"If it cleared up by itself, Ni Ni could have stayed here," I said. After the words came out of my mouth, I was sorry.

Mom cleared her throat and started reading the letter out loud. I buried my hands in the keys and listened. "'Ni Ni is not adjusting as quickly to California as I thought she would. Most of the time she wants to stay in her room. This spring has

been unusually cold. She says she prefers to stay home and sort through her newspaper articles. She says she is saving them for when Xiao Jimmy comes to visit. So, enclosed is a ticket for Jimmy. This way he can be here for her eightieth birthday. Love to all, Helen.'" Mom handed me the ticket. On the top it said, *Ticket holder: Jimmy Wu. Destination: San Francisco.*

I looked at Mom. "Can I really go? To California? By myself?"

Mom didn't answer at first. She was reading the letter again. Then she folded it and put it back into the envelope. "I know Dad will say that's the best birthday present we can give Ni Ni." She handed the envelope to me and I read the ticket over and over.

CHAPTER ELEVEN

A Gift for Ni Ni

I tried hard to think of a birthday gift for Ni Ni. Mom and I wandered around in a department store. "Maybe she would like some kitchen towels," Mom suggested.

I shook my head. They all had flowers on them. They didn't look like the kind of towels Ni Ni had in her kitchen. We went to the Chinese food store.

Mom thought Ni Ni might like a nice pair of chopsticks.

"Ni Ni already has so many chopsticks," I said.

"But these are special red ones for holidays," Mom told me, holding them up.

"Ni Ni will never use them." I shrugged. "She'll use the old pairs and save the new ones and never take them out of the box." Mom went back and bought the towels for Auntie Helen, and we went home with nothing for Ni Ni. I stayed outside to shoot baskets with Jason.

"Guess what?" I told him. "My aunt sent me a ticket to California."

"She did?" Jason was so surprised, he stopped dribbling.

"Yup."

"Are you going by yourself?"

"Yup. It's a gift for my grandma's birthday."

Jason looked hard at me. "Did you say your aunt got you a ticket for your grandma's birthday?"

I nodded.

Jason shook his head. "For my grandma's birthday, I bought her a candy dish out of real crystal. My mom said it was too expensive, but with all this baby-sitting, I figured I could afford it. What are you going to get for your grandma?"

"I'm not sure. There's nothing I think she'd really like."

"I can show you where I got that candy dish if you want."

"My grandma never eats candy."

"You know, Jimmy, I just don't get it. Sometimes I think you've got the weirdest family."

I felt the blood rush to my face just like it did in

second grade when all the kids started calling me crybaby. My throat swelled. I swallowed hard. Then I looked right into Jason's eyes and said, "Your family isn't perfect either."

"Never said it was."

"You don't even want to visit your grandma, and I think that's about the weirdest thing I've ever heard."

"Well, you don't even know my family because you're just too scared to come over to my house."

"I am not."

"Then why do you always make up some excuse? 'I have to help my grandma.'" Jason copied my high voice. "Well, your grandma's not here anymore."

"Let's go, then," I said.

Jason looked surprised. "Right now?"

I nodded. We didn't say a word as we walked. Then right before we got to his door, Jason turned to me. "Sorry," he said quietly, and then headed into the house and straight down to the basement. It was dark and musty. There was an old couch facing a big television set that was on. In the middle of the room was the Ping-Pong table. Jason picked up a paddle and handed me one.

"I don't know how to play," I said.

"You just hit the ball over the net, that's all." I stood on the side of the table facing the television set. Jason served the ball slowly so it bounced right in front of me. I hit it, but it went off the end of the table.

"Pretty good. Just hit softer," Jason said. He served again. I smacked the ball so high, it almost hit the ceiling, but it still bounced onto his side of the table. We hit the ball back and forth five times before I missed.

"You're good for a beginner," Jason said, starting over again.

After a while, Jason's mother came down and turned off the television. "Hi, Jimmy." She set a basket of laundry on the floor. "How's your grandma like California?"

"I'm not sure," I answered.

"Moving is always hard, especially at her age." Then she put the clothes into the washing machine and went back upstairs.

Without the television on, the basement seemed really dark. The only sound was the water sloshing around in the washing machine. "Want to see my room?" Jason asked.

"Sure." Jason's room was small like mine, but

much messier, with Legos all over the floor. We scooped them into a pile and started building. I made a robot; Jason made a time machine. His machine could take you into the past or the future. My robot was from another planet. We kept adding more and more pieces. "I wouldn't mind going back to see my great-grandpa in the Civil War," Jason said.

"I wouldn't mind going back to see how my grandma's brother got stuck in a closet in Shanghai."

"Stuck in a closet?"

"Yeah. You know that jar of keys I have? One of them is to that closet."

"You mean it came all the way from China?"

"Yup."

"Pretty cool. Hey, you want to see something really old?" Jason took a shoe box off the shelf.

Inside were all kinds of fossils. "Brachiopods, bryo-zoans, and this one's a trilobite."

We sorted the fossils for a while. Jason knew all about how they were formed millions of years ago. I glanced at the clock on the wall. Five o'clock. Almost the whole afternoon had gone by. "I better go. My mom will be wondering where I am."

"Oh, I almost forgot, I found something for you at my grandma's," Jason said. He reached into his pocket and held out a key.

"Did you ask her what it's for?"

"She said it was to my grandpa's old desk."

"Where's the desk now?"

"After he died, she gave the desk away. It made her sad every time she looked at it. Then she showed me all this stuff that used to be in my grandpa's desk, like a pocket watch that flips open. She said that someday it'll be mine." I took the key from Jason. "I told my grandma about your key collection, and she said she might have some more for you next time we go."

"Tell her thanks," I said.

Jason walked home with me. The afternoon sun was so strong, you could see the heat rising off the blacktop in waves. "I bet it'll be even hotter in California," Jason said. We went to the kitchen for a drink of water. Jason saw our chopsticks drying on the dish rack. "Is it hard to eat with those?" he asked.

"Not really." Jason took two chopsticks and tried to hold them in one hand. I showed him how to position the bottom one like a pencil and then move the top one to it, but he kept dropping the bottom one. "When I was little, my grandma used to tie them together with a rubber band to make it easier," I said. I took a rubber band off the windowsill and wound it around two chopsticks. I wadded a tissue in between the two sticks. Jason tried again.

"That's more like it," he said.

We sat on the living-room rug. I added Jason's grandma's key to the jar. Then we dumped out all the keys. Jason tried to pick them up with the chopsticks. At first he kept dropping them, but finally he got a few back into the jar.

"You're pretty good for a beginner," I said, and smiled. Then I showed Jason the key to Ni Ni's trunk.

He picked it up. "It's a little bent."

"Still works, though." I told him how I found Ni Ni's quilt inside the trunk.

"Did your grandma take the trunk with her to California?"

"Yup."

"That means she can't open it," Jason said, "because you've got the key." I'd never even thought of that. Ni Ni's quilt was locked up again.

"Hey, now I know what to give my grandma for her birthday." I picked up the bent key with my chopsticks and dropped it into the jar.

CHAPTER TWELVE
California

Our last day of school was May 31, and on June 1, I packed everything I thought I'd need in California. Pants, T-shirts, my toothbrush. Mom helped me fold my clothes and put them into the small suitcase. We wrapped the key collection in some dish towels and put it in the middle of the shirts.

Jason was at the door. "Could you please give this to your grandma?" he asked. He had a big envelope. In it was a recipe from his mother for chocolate chip cookies and a picture of the Greek zodiac signs that he had drawn. "I thought she might like to know about our zodiac, along with the Chinese one," he said.

"Thanks," I told him. Jason stood there for a minute. Alice came outside with one baby on each hip. "Wave bye-bye to Jimmy," she told the boys. "You have a nice trip, Jimmy. Tell your grandma we hope to meet her sometime."

❊

The airport was crowded. Mom kept looking at her watch until finally they said it was time to board. My stomach flipped. What if I got lost in

California? What if nobody was waiting for me at the airport?

Mom and Dad gave me hugs. "Tell Ni Ni we said happy birthday," Dad said. Mom didn't say anything at all. I took my place in the line of people. When it was my turn, I put my ticket into the slot, grabbed the stub, and walked slowly down the ramp.

Everything looked so small from inside the airplane. I could see the curve of the earth where it met the sky. Someday I would go up in a rocket and see the whole world from above. The plane went up and down; my stomach dropped. The air vent blew cold air on my head and I shivered. The man next to me was reading the newspaper. He didn't seem worried at all. I opened the book I'd brought, but my eyes wouldn't focus on the words. I did

Ni Ni's eye exercises, but they didn't seem to help. I took out my notebook and a pen from my book bag and practiced writing the few Chinese characters I knew. I would ask Ni Ni to teach me more. Jason wanted to know how to write his name in Chinese. Ni Ni could show me. I must have fallen asleep, because when I woke up, the wheels of the plane were bumping along the ground.

Ni Ni and Auntie Helen were the first ones behind the blue rope. I saw their faces looking at the crowd, but they didn't see me yet. I started running, not caring if I bumped into anyone. My book bag was bouncing on my back, up and down, faster and faster. When I reached Ni Ni, she hugged me like she would never let go. She had the same smell as the kitchen of her old house. She held on to me even when we started to walk. "Xiao

Jimmy is not so *xiao* anymore," Auntie Helen said. She was right. I was almost as tall as both of them.

"Drink lot milk, Xiao Jimmy," Ni Ni said.

When we got to Auntie Helen's, Ni Ni took me right to her room. For a minute, I thought I was in her old house. Same bed, same desk, same trunk. I put my suitcase on the bed and unzipped it.

"I brought you something, Ni Ni."

"Bring yourself is enough."

"But I brought you something else." I reached into the suitcase and pulled out the jar of keys. "Happy birthday, Ni Ni," I said.

"So heavy to carry all the keys, Xiao Jimmy," Ni Ni said, smiling.

We dumped them on her bed. I showed Ni Ni the four-leaf-clover key from the real estate lady, the key that baby Rob found, and the newest one, from Jason's grandpa's desk. Then I picked up the Ni Ni key and took it over to the trunk. I turned it in the lock and the latch sprung.

"Bent key still works," Ni Ni said. Together we took out the quilt and spread it on the bed. "You know, Xiao Jimmy, I think you take this quilt back to Cincinnati when you go home."

"But your mom made it for you."

"In California, no need for quilt."

I lay down and felt the cool silk on my cheeks. Ni Ni sat down beside me. We traced the butterflies. I liked the red one with wings spread out near the edge of the quilt. Ni Ni said that she liked the yellow one resting on a twig. Then my stomach growled.

"Po hear that," Ni Ni said as she grabbed my hand. We headed into the kitchen.

That night, Auntie Helen put a cot for me next to Ni Ni's bed. "I bet your window is just in line with mine," I said.

"But so many mountains in the middle." Ni Ni looked out the window.

"Still, we see the same moon." The moon was just rising on the horizon. "The moon told me you have been staying up too late," I teased.

"The moon told me same thing," Ni Ni said.

We talked until way past midnight. I told Ni Ni about Rob and Mark and Jason. I told her that I went to Jason's house. "What did you do there?" Ni Ni asked.

"First we played Ping-Pong."

"Jason a nice boy," Ni Ni said.

I nodded in the dark. "I used to be kind of scared to go to his house."

"Get used to everything takes long time," Ni Ni said quietly.

⌖

In the morning, Ni Ni taught me some new Chinese characters: *airplane, mama, friend.* I practiced writing them on squared paper. I asked Ni Ni if she could write Jason in Chinese. "Jason," Ni Ni said. "*Jie Sen.*" Then she took out a calligraphy brush, dipped it carefully into the ink, and made the first bold stroke. Her arm moved smoothly as she worked, just like Jason when he shoveled snow. Ni Ni said the first character, *jie*, meant "outstanding," and the second one, *sen*, meant "forest." Outstanding forest. I couldn't wait to tell Jason.

I practiced writing the characters for "friend," *peng you*, on my squared paper. Ni Ni said my strokes were just right. When I got home, I would teach Jason. When Rob and Mark got big, maybe I would teach them too.

That afternoon, Auntie Helen suggested that Ni Ni and I take a walk to the library. It was only about three blocks away. Ni Ni shook her head. "Too old to explore," she said. Then she shivered. "Anyway, too cold today." Auntie Helen looked at me.

"But Ni Ni, you've only had one birthday, remember?" I looked out the window. The sun was bright and strong. "And it's warm outside."

I could see Ni Ni trying to come up with an excuse, just like I had done when Jason asked me to go over to his house. "You go, Xiao Jimmy, I wait for you."

"I don't want to go by myself," I said as I helped Ni Ni put on her sweater. "Now you'll be warm." I took her arm and guided her out the door. The air was cool, but the sun was hot on our backs. Across the street the valley was full of fog. If you looked past it and squinted, you could catch a glimpse of the ocean.

When we got to the library, I helped Ni Ni fill out the form for a library card. "So you can take out any book you want." I picked up a big book with a rocket on the cover.

Ni Ni didn't touch the books. "All in English," she said.

"But you can read some English. And they have pictures too." I found a big book called *China in Pictures*. We sat together and looked at the chapter on Shanghai.

"So different," Ni Ni said, looking at a photo-

graph of the Pearl Tower. "Not like old Shanghai."
We stayed a long time, staring at all the pictures.
Ni Ni told me what looked the same and what had
changed. On a city map, she showed me where she
used to live and where Po lived now.

On our way out of the library, I picked up a
pamphlet about free English classes on Wednesday
mornings. I showed it to Ni Ni. "You know, Xiao
Jimmy, now I'm too old to learn English," Ni Ni
said.

The librarian heard us. "I don't think so. We
have one woman in the class who is ninety-four."
She held a clipboard out to Ni Ni so she could add
her name to the list. Ni Ni hesitated and looked
at me.

"That other lady is much older than you are,"
I said.

Shu Yuan Wu, Ni Ni wrote carefully on the line.

"See you Wednesday," the librarian said.

When we got home, Auntie Helen had fixed a special lunch for Ni Ni's birthday. "I know it won't be your real birthday for forty more years, but still," she said, giving us each a scoop of steamed rice and broccoli and Ni Ni's favorite shrimp. Then she handed Ni Ni a letter that had come from Shanghai. Ni Ni looked at the return address.

"From Po."

I went to get the big flat key so we could slit the envelope without damaging the stamps. Ni Ni set the letter down between us on the table and read it out loud. All of a sudden I realized that I knew enough characters to follow along. I saw the characters for *airplane* over and over. I listened to what Po had written. He wanted Ni Ni to celebrate her eightieth birthday with her brothers in Shanghai this winter. At the end he wrote, *Please bring Xiao Jimmy with you.*

I looked at Auntie Helen. "Does he really mean it?"

"Of course he does."

"Do you think Mom and Dad will let me go during my winter break?"

"Of course," said Ni Ni. "Old lady all alone cannot go."

Auntie Helen nodded. "Ni Ni is right. Later we'll call Mom and Dad."

⌘

After lunch, Ni Ni and I spread the quilt on her bed and dumped the key collection onto it. "Can we take all the keys to Shanghai?" I asked. "Maybe your brothers remember what some of them are for."

Ni Ni nodded. "I know Po remember this one," she said, holding up the Xiao Jimmy key.

"Jason likes this one," I said, "with the four-leaf clover on top for good luck."

"I am the one with good luck." Ni Ni patted my head.

I felt the butterflies with my finger. I imagined Ni Ni's mother making all the tiny stitches in red and green and gold. Then I imagined Ni Ni and me sitting together on a big airplane, flying across the whole Pacific Ocean.

"Ni Ni."

"Hmmm."

"How long will it take us to get to Shanghai?"

"Maybe fifteen hours. Maybe more."

I smiled. "Good. We can play rock-paper-scissors."

Ni Ni nodded.

"And you can teach me more Chinese characters."

"Better you teach me English."

"Will they give us dinner on the plane?"

"Yes. Breakfast too."

"Maybe we better pack some *jiao zi*, just in case."

"Good idea, Xiao Jimmy." Ni Ni held my hands in her wrinkled ones. "Just in case."

How to Make Jiao Zi

Filling

2 pounds ground meat (pork is best, but ground shrimp or
   another ground meat is fine)

2 tablespoons soy sauce

2 teaspoons salt

2 teaspoons black pepper

1 teaspoon sesame oil

2 cloves crushed garlic

   pinch of sugar

Combine all ingredients in a bowl. Then mix in the
following:

3–4 green onions, finely minced

1 small head Chinese cabbage or bok choy, finely chopped

Wrappers

approximately 1 cup cold water

2½ cups flour

Add water to flour and blend to form stiff dough. If dough is too soft, add more flour. Knead thoroughly. Form dough into two long sausages, about an inch in diameter. Pull off small pieces and form into about 50 balls. Then use a rolling pin or wooden dowel to flatten each ball into a circle about three inches in diameter. (Pot sticker wrappers can also be purchased in many supermarkets or in Asian specialty shops.)

Dumplings

To form dumplings, place approximately one tablespoon of filling in the center of each wrapper. Fold dough in half and pinch closed using water as glue. (They look especially nice if the top half is "pleated.")

Cooking Jiao Zi

Jiao zi can be boiled or panfried.

To BOIL: Bring a large pot of water to boil and add jiao zi. Boil for ten minutes or until meat in center is cooked thoroughly. Remove dumplings with slotted spoon and serve.

To panfry: Heat 1 to 2 tablespoons vegetable oil in skillet. Add *jiao zi* (only a single layer should be fried at a time) and cook until bottoms are brown. Add enough cold water to barely cover *jiao zi* and place lid on pan. When water comes to boil, add another cup of cold water. Add cold water three times until all water is absorbed and *jiao zi* are done, approximately 10 to 15 minutes.

Serve with soy sauce and rice vinegar or dipping sauce, below.

Dipping Sauce

$1/4$ *cup soy sauce*

2 tablespoons vinegar, preferably rice vinegar

$1/2$ *teaspoon sugar (or to taste)*

Jiao zi are easy to freeze. Before cooking, place dumplings on a tray so that they are not touching. Put into freezer. The next day, transfer dumplings to plastic bags.

Pronunciation Guide and Glossary

jiao zi (jiow dze): a type of Chinese dumpling

jie (ji-eh): outstanding

jie jie (ji-eh ji-eh): big sister

peng you (pung yo): friend

sen (sun): forest

xiao (sheow): little

xiao mei (sheow may): little sister

xie xie (shie shie): thank you

Numbers

yi (ee): one

er (are): two

san (san): three

si (seh): four

wu (woo): five

liu (leo): six

qi (chee): seven

ba (ba): eight